Ghost Woman on a White Horse

Caitlin didn't want to hear about ghosts from Mr. Giles. It was scary enough in that mine tunnel, with spooky shadows dancing on the walls as the kids' flashlights swung back and forth in their hands.

"Well," Mr. Giles began again, "the way the miners tell it, one day they were lowering a new horse—a white one—down the shaft to work in the mines. Miners saw it go past at the six hundred- and nine hundred-foot levels. But when the hoist got down to the fifteen hundred-foot level, the sling was empty. The white horse was gone."

The whole group stopped walking now. They clustered around Mr. Giles.

"What happened to the white horse?" Caitlin asked.

"For years and years, miners kept seeing it in one tunnel after another, deep inside the mine. And someone was always riding it. A woman. Dressed in a flowing white gown. They say her husband died in the mine, and she kept calling him, searching for his body. But whenever one of the miners tried to talk to her, she vanished. In thin air."

MYSTERY OF THE HAUNTED SILVER MINE

by Gloria Skurzynski & Alane Ferguson

illustrated by Jeffrey Lindberg

For Lauren and Andrew,
our favorite couple

CHAPTER 1

"Reese Borden, that is *not* true! The silver mine isn't haunted," Lily Kato said, her voice quavering.

Caitlin Marsh put her arm around Lily's thin shoulder and hugged her friend as tightly as she could. "Yeah, Reese," Caitlin echoed. "There aren't any ghosts in there." And then, so that Reese wouldn't think the stories bothered *her*, Caitlin added, "Quit trying to scare Lily."

The entire Science Club stood in front of Three Peaks Elementary School, waiting for their teacher, Mr. Mahoney. He and three adult chaperons were going to take them on a field trip to the abandoned silver mine. They had flashlights and small rock hammers to chip bits of ore out of the mine walls. They also had magnifying glasses to examine the samples and a hand scale to weigh them. That is, Mr. Mahoney had the hand scale. But he hadn't come yet. For some reason, he was late. To pass the time, obnoxious Reese kept yakking about spirits who prowled the dark mine shafts.

"The ghosts of the dead miners take their lights in their hands, like this . . ." Reese raised his hands over his head, pretending to hold up a lantern. Since Reese starred in real-life movies, he was always acting things out. "The ghosts float through the old silver mine, calling 'Ooooh, ooooh, someone come find me.' But they don't ever come out of the mine. Do you know why?"

"Why?" Lily gasped.

Reese leaned closer, his voice barely a whisper. "Because they can't leave their dry, crushed bones behind, underneath the fallen rocks in the mine. They have to stay there with their bones and haunt the mine—*forever*!"

Suddenly, Caitlin felt an icy hand grab her by the back of the neck. She leaped into the air, and Lily screamed.

"Gotcha!" Pablo Miramontes laughed and gave Reese a high-five. Reese was laughing even louder than Pablo.

"That was no ghost; it was me—Pablo the funny-man," he bragged. "I put my hand around a cold can of soda so it would feel clammy and *dead*. Then I grabbed your neck. You thought it was a ghost."

"No, I didn't. There's no such thing as ghosts!" Caitlin declared, although she was still shaking inside.

"Oh, yeah? I know for sure there are ghosts in that mine," Pablo insisted. "My cousin Marcus rode past there on his bike one day last week, and he saw a light. Not only that—" Pablo leaned close to Lily, just the way Reese had done. "Marcus heard howls, like this . . . ow-ooooo! And screeches coming from inside!"

Sixth-grader Joe Daniel Giles, the boy Caitlin liked the best, rolled his eyes at Reese and Pablo. "Come on, you guys, give us a break," he scoffed. "Mr. Mahoney already told us that all that ghost stuff is just a legend. The only thing scaring me is Mr. Mahoney being so late." He glanced at his wristwatch. "It's already three-thirty. He should have been here by now."

Wind rattled the early fall leaves and sent them sailing like tiny golden kites. It was chilly outside. Caitlin wished their teacher would drive up in the school's small yellow bus. And then, as if wishing made it so, the bus rumbled into view. Caitlin watched as Mr. Mahoney pulled to a stop, set the brake, pushed the handle that opened the door, and clambered down to the parking lot.

"Sorry I'm late, kids," he apologized, looking grim. "I'm afraid we've got ourselves a problem. A big problem! My student teacher couldn't make the trip, one of the parent volunteers called in sick, and the other one couldn't get a baby-sitter. That leaves just me to watch over all of you."

"We'll be okay—" Joe Daniel began, but Mr. Mahoney interrupted.

"That old silver mine can be dangerous," he said. "I realize how much you were all looking forward to gathering rock samples in a real mine, and you've done a lot of research to get ready. But without another adult to go along with us, we'll just have to cancel the trip. I'm really sorry."

"No!" Caitlin cried in dismay. The other Science Club members were just as unhappy.

"Please let us go!" Chantelle Landers, a fifth-grader, begged. "We promise we'll stay together!"

There was a chorus of "Come on, give us a chance," and "I bought a new flashlight just for today."

Reese stomped his foot. "I turned down an interview with *Starz* magazine to go on this trip. I want to see some *ghosts*."

"What ghosts! Forget it, Reese," Joe Daniel said. "Mr. Mahoney, I could help you watch out for the kids."

The teacher shook his head. "I know you're reliable, Joe Daniel, but you're still a student at Three Peaks Elementary. We have to have grown-ups along."

Caitlin felt as disappointed as the rest of her friends. She wished her mother, who had gone into town to run errands today, could go with them. But there was no way Caitlin could get in touch with her.

Mr. Mahoney was saying, "I'd get into a lot of trouble if a parent asked me who was in charge of this tour and I had to answer, me—and one student, Joe Daniel Giles."

Suddenly, Caitlin had a great idea. Leaning close to Joe Daniel, she whispered in his ear.

She knew just the person who could take them to the old silver mine. If she was right, the trip could be saved!

CHAPTER 2

By four-thirty they'd reached the mine.

"I'm certainly glad you invited me on this trip, Caitlin," Mr. Giles said as they climbed down from the minibus.

It had been Caitlin's idea to get Joe Daniel's grandfather for a chaperon. Mr. Giles owned the ranch where Caitlin and her mother rented their trailer space. In autumn, after all the hay had been cut and stacked, ranchers had a little extra time to do things— like go along on school field trips.

Everyone stood beside the empty bus while Mr. Mahoney checked off their names on his list. "Chantelle, Paige, Caitlin, Lily," he called out, starting with the girls. Then, "Joe Daniel, Reese, Jeremiah, Kevin, Pablo."

"I'm not here," Pablo said in his usual joking way.

"Well, I'm going to count you anyway," Mr. Mahoney said. "Boys and girls, we're really lucky to have Mr. Giles with us on our expedition. He knows a lot about this old silver mine, and about how the workers brought out ore."

"My granddaddy was a Welsh miner," Mr. Giles announced.

"What's a 'well shminer'?" Caitlin asked, interested.

10

Maybe it was someone who drilled wells to get water. There was a well right outside the Giles' ranch house.

"Welsh . . . miner." Speaking slowly, Joe Daniel corrected Caitlin. "That means he came from Wales."

"Oh." Caitlin still didn't understand, but she nodded as if she did. She hated to look dumb in front of Joe Daniel.

"Yes," Mr. Giles went on, "my granddaddy told me stories I'll never forget, not as long as I live."

"I wish I remembered things better," Caitlin said, searching the inside of her backpack. "Sometimes I forget things. Like . . ." She ran her hand through the backpack a second time, then bit the side of her lip. ". . . my flashlight. I . . . I think I left it on my bed."

Suddenly, Mr. Mahoney appeared next to where Caitlin stood. "Excuse me, but did you say you forgot your flashlight?" he demanded.

Uh-oh! "Yes," Caitlin had to admit.

"Oh, Caitlin!" Mr. Mahoney sighed, shaking his head. "Here we are, all ready to go into the mine, and you don't have a flashlight. What are we going to do with you?"

"I'm sorry!" She'd really, truly tried to remember everything she was supposed to bring for the mine exploration. She had her water bottle in her backpack, along with an apple for a snack. She was wearing both her red sweatshirt and her denim jacket, because Mr. Mahoney had warned them that the mine would be no warmer than fifty-five degrees inside. And she had on sturdy shoes.

"I can share my flashlight with Caitlin," Lily offered. "I've got a good one, see?" She held up a

11

sturdy-looking red flashlight that she clicked on and off to show how brightly it shone.

Lily was so nice! She was a bit timid, but that was okay, Caitlin thought. Lily always dressed in pretty colors and wore big bows in her hair. Today, a pale silk scarf tied back her straight black ponytail.

"All right," Mr. Mahoney decided. "You two girls may share a single flashlight. But you must stick together every minute! Do you understand?"

"Yes," Caitlin answered.

"Yes," Lily agreed.

"Never leave each other's side!" Mr. Mahoney ordered.

"We won't! We'll stick—" Lily began.

"—like Super Glue!" Caitlin finished.

"Okay, everyone, line up here while I give you instructions," Mr. Mahoney called out.

When all had gathered around, Mr. Mahoney began speaking. "First," he said, "I want you to look at this mine entrance. You'll have to stoop to get inside. Since the mine closed thirty years ago, dirt and rock have partly blocked the way in."

It looked like a cave for dwarfs. But Mr. Mahoney had told them that on the inside, tunnels branched off in all different directions for miles and miles.

"We're only going to walk about a quarter of a mile in the mine," Mr. Mahoney went on. "Just so you can follow the seam of ore in the matrix—that means surrounding rock—and get an idea of what it looks like. Also, when we're far enough along that we can no longer see light from the mine entrance, we're going to turn off our flashlights for just one minute. To let you experience absolute darkness."

Caitlin nodded. He'd said all this before, in class.

"What's the main rule?" Mr. Mahoney asked them.

"Stay together!" they all shouted.

"Does everyone have a buddy?"

"Yes!" Caitlin grabbed Lily's hand and lifted it into the air, to show Mr. Mahoney they would stick together like Super Glue.

"Then let's go!"

CHAPTER 3

"It really is dark in here!" Caitlin exclaimed.

"Just be glad we have flashlights," Mr. Mahoney told the kids. "Back in the old days, miners used candles and got only three a day to last them for a whole ten hours underground. They'd nail tin cans to the wooden beams, like these"—he gestured at the thick posts lining the walls and ceiling—"to hold spare candles and matches. Sometimes their candles melted down too fast."

"What would make a candle do that?" Joe Daniel asked.

Mr. Mahoney told them, "Lots of air from a draft. You can feel the fresh breeze blowing through from the mine entrance. That makes it nice and dry right here where we're standing. But if we went deeper into the mine, to the six hundred- and nine hundred- and fifteen hundred-foot levels, you'd see water dripping down the walls."

They started out two by two, following Mr. Mahoney. Mr. Giles stayed at the very back of the line to make sure no one got separated from the group. From the front of the line, Mr. Mahoney explained things in a loud voice as they went, shining his flashlight on the sides of the tunnel to show specks of ore in the rock. "See this?" he said, pointing to a seam.

14

"Who can tell me what kind of rock this is?"

"Mostly limestone and quartz," Joe Daniel answered. Joe Daniel knew more about science than any of the other kids in the club. He didn't talk a lot, but when he did, he was worth listening to.

Mr. Giles, Joe Daniel's grandfather, *did* talk a lot. He seemed to enjoy telling the kids about the old days, when miners rode in cages down a shaft into the deepest levels of the mine.

"And not only miners," he told them. "They took horses down there, too, to pull the ore cars. A hoist lowered the horses in slings, all the way down the shaft to the fifteen hundred-foot level. They built regular stables down there for the horses."

"What did the horses eat?" Caitlin asked. She couldn't imagine grass growing that deep in a silver mine.

"Hay," Mr. Giles answered. "It got lowered in bales on a special wooden platform that ran on pulleys. The horses ate grain, too. And mice would often be hiding in the bags of grain, so the miners brought down cats to catch the mice. At night, the cats would sleep on the horses' backs to keep warm—"

Just at that moment Pablo popped out at them. He held his flashlight right under his face. It made his chin red and painted dark shadows under his lips, nose, and eyebrows. He looked so spooky that Lily jumped.

"Pablo, get back in line with your partner," Mr. Mahoney ordered him.

"I will. But first I want to know—are there any ghosts in this mine, Mr. Giles?"

"Of course not," Mr. Mahoney said from the front of the line.

From the back of the line, Mr. Giles said, "Well . . ."

Pablo danced with excitement. His flashlight beam jiggled up and down. "I knew it! I knew there had to be ghosts in here," he said. "Tell us about them!"

"Oh, they're probably just stories the miners made up," Mr. Giles replied.

"I don't care. I want to hear them," Pablo insisted. His partner, Reese, chimed in, "Me, too. Please tell us, Mr. Giles."

Caitlin didn't want to hear about ghosts. It was scary enough in that mine tunnel, with spooky shadows dancing on the walls as the kids' flashlights swung back and forth in their hands. Lily squeezed Caitlin's arm so tightly that Caitlin nearly cried "Ouch," but she didn't want to make Lily any more upset than she already was.

"Well," Mr. Giles began again, "the way the miners tell it, one day they were lowering a new horse—a white horse—down the shaft to work in the mines. The miners saw it go past the tunnel at the six hundred-foot level. Other miners saw it drop past the tunnel at nine hundred feet. But when the hoist got down to the fifteen hundred-foot level, the sling was empty. The white horse was gone."

The whole group had stopped walking now. They clustered around Mr. Giles, pointing their flashlights down so the light wouldn't shine in his eyes.

"What happened to the white horse?" Caitlin asked.

"For years and years, miners kept seeing it in one tunnel after another, deep inside the mine." Mr. Giles's voice got lower and softer. "And someone was always riding it. A woman. Dressed in a flowing white gown. They say her husband died in the mine, and she kept calling him, searching for his body, which was never found. But whenever one of the miners tried to talk to her, she vanished. Into thin air."

"Ooooh," the girls squealed. Some of the boys looked a little scared, too.

"I bet lots of miners died in here, right?" Reese Borden asked.

"Reese . . ." Mr. Mahoney warned.

"There was a big explosion once," Mr. Giles went on, not catching Mr. Mahoney's signal to stop telling scary stories. "The blast was so powerful, it blew the hair right off the miners' heads. They said the hair shot into the wooden support beams that hold up the walls of these tunnels. Some people say it's still there, stuck in the beams. And that . . . the hair's *still growing*!"

"Let's get moving now, boys and girls," Mr. Mahoney interrupted, shepherding them into line again. "Mr. Giles, would you come up front with me for a minute? I think we need to talk."

That left Lily and Caitlin at the very back of the group. At least that's what Caitlin thought, until she heard whispers behind her. Then Lily screamed.

"Something's on me! What is it?" Lily cried.

Caitlin grabbed the flashlight as Lily yelled and pulled at the side of her neck. When Caitlin shone the light on Lily's neck, she saw a smeary blob of green goo. She tried to pull it off, but it was cold and slimy, like the underside of a slug.

"Don't move, Lily," Caitlin commanded. "I'll get it off! It's just so . . . squishy!"

"Hurry!" Lily screamed. "It's *gross*!"

Suddenly, Caitlin felt a glop of the same slimy

green goo land squarely on her cheek. Wildly, she searched in the darkness, trying to find the source of the slithery stuff.

"Oh, no—what happened to you guys?" Pablo asked, shining his flashlight right on her face. "Did you get slimed by a ghost? Ha ha ha!"

Caitlin saw it then, a small, clear plastic case nestled in the palm of Pablo's hand—the kind you could buy for a quarter from a vending machine at the grocery store, the kind that was full of disgusting green jelly slime.

"Here now, what's going on with you girls?" Mr. Mahoney called back from the head of the line. "Is something wrong?"

Before Lily could say a word, Caitlin shouted, "No, nothing. Not a thing. Lily and I are *just* fine."

"Why didn't you tell him?" Lily whispered. "I *want* Pablo and Reese to get into trouble."

"I've got a better idea," Caitlin said softly, taking Lily's arm. "They've just played their last joke. 'Cause now, it's *our* turn!"

CHAPTER 4

"Minerals in the walls," Mr. Mahoney was telling the group gathered around him. "We'll chip some samples here, and then we'll move down to that tunnel on the left. Now, take out your hammers and tap off a bit of rock. We can examine it more closely tomorrow in school."

"You ready?" Caitlin whispered.

Lily nodded silently.

Even though it was hard to see much in the shadowy silver mine, Caitlin could tell that Lily was a little afraid. She'd never played a joke on anyone before, not in her whole entire life. But then again, she'd never had slime thrown on her neck before, either.

Tink, tink, tink. The sounds of the hammers echoed like musical notes. Caitlin grinned, picturing Pablo's face when she and Lily played *their* trick. Although Caitlin's mother had always taught her that it was better to be nice than to get even, just this once, Caitlin thought, she'd like to try it the other way around.

While the rest of the Science Club tapped the rock, Caitlin, followed by Lily, crept along the bumpy wall. Just ahead, the mine shaft split like a capital letter Y. Caitlin's plan was to stay to the left. Mr. Mahoney had already told the kids they'd be walking in that direction. Once Caitlin and Lily reached the second tunnel, they'd hide and wait for Pablo and Reese to walk by with the rest of the club. Then, right when the boys passed in front of them, Caitlin and Lily would jump out and scare them. It would serve them right!

Glancing over her shoulder, Caitlin could see the beams of the flashlights bobbing like fireflies. No one had noticed the two girls slipping away. They tiptoed a little farther, and then farther. . . .

"There's not much valuable ore, at least not in this main tunnel. Miners took it out long ago. They'd put the ore in carts that ran on tracks, but all the tracks are covered up now by rubble and fallen rocks." Mr. Mahoney began to sound farther away. "I see Reese has got a bit of silver fever. No, no, Reese—don't hit it so hard. The glitter is just tiny flakes of silver. All put together, it wouldn't make up half of what's in a dime."

The voices grew muffled as Caitlin and Lily scurried around the corner into the left-hand tunnel. They'd made it! A rush of cool air wrapped around them. Caitlin felt the chill, even through her sweatshirt. Without the other flashlights to light the way, the darkness in front of them seemed to yawn like a huge black hole.

"Are you sure we're not going to get in trouble?" Lily whispered. "We're pretty far away from the rest of the Science Club."

"I know what I'm doing," Caitlin whispered back. "They'll come this way any second. Pablo's going to be *so* sorry he messed with us! Reese, too."

"But—"

Caitlin grabbed Lily by the hand and pulled. "Don't be a weenie. Come on!"

The small circle of Lily's light danced across the ceiling and the floor. On either side of the tunnel, large beams stood like wooden guards along the walls. Old chain-link fencing had been nailed into the ceiling to keep rocks from raining down. Everything in the tunnel was either black, gray, or brown. To Caitlin it almost seemed as if they'd stepped inside an old black-and-white television set.

"This is spooky," Lily murmured.

"I know." Grinning, Caitlin added, "It's perfect for payback. When Pablo and Reese walk by, we'll scare them soooo bad!"

Nodding, Lily declared, "They deserve it."

The beam of light suddenly dipped into a small hollow in the wall thirty feet ahead of them. "Hey, look! We can hide in that little cubbyhole over there, and they'll never see us."

"Wait a minute, Caitlin," Lily protested. "I don't want to get lost—"

"We know exactly where we are. Come on, Lily, I think I hear them coming!" The sounds of footsteps rattled along the rock walls.

"Hurry!" Caitlin cried. When they reached the hiding spot, she whispered to Lily, "Turn off your flashlight."

Inky blackness covered them like a blanket. Caitlin couldn't see anything at all, not even the barest outline of Lily's head, even though the two of them were squeezed tightly together in the narrow groove in the wall.

"Caitlin!" That voice belonged to Mr. Giles. "Where are you?"

"I think Caitlin and Lily went up to the front of the line," Chantelle answered.

23

Caitlin stifled a giggle. The sounds were getting closer and closer—footsteps crunching on the gravel floor. Any minute, just before the other kids' lights brightened the tunnel, Lily and Caitlin would bounce out and scare Reese and Pablo.

"This is going to be so funny!" Caitlin whispered.

And then, as if someone were slowly turning down a radio, the voices got softer instead of louder. No flashlight beams skipped along the rocky walls. No shoes shuffled on the pebbly earth. Just faint—very faint—echoes reached them from far, far away.

"No one's coming in here!" Lily hissed.

"They will. They've got to. Just wait, they'll come."

Another minute crept by, and then another. The smile drained from Caitlin's face. Two important things had gone wrong: First, the Science Club kids hadn't walked in the direction they were supposed to, so Lily's and Caitlin's joke was ruined.

The second problem was even worse: Mr. Mahoney would probably find out that the two girls had strayed from the group. It wouldn't matter to him one bit that they were just trying to pay back Pablo and Reese. No matter what, Caitlin knew that she and Lily were in for some pretty serious scolding.

Maybe if they waited just a little longer, the group would turn around and come back toward them. Then Caitlin and Lily could slip in with everyone else and pretend they hadn't been gone at all.

One little second, two little seconds. Caitlin counted off the time in her head. By the time she reached "sixty little seconds," it seemed that far more than a minute must have gone by. "I . . . I guess you're right, Lily," she said finally. "We'd better catch up to

24

them. Go ahead and turn on your flashlight."

There was a click.

"Come on, turn it on," Caitlin commanded.

"I did!" Lily said, her voice shaking. "It's not working!"

"What?" Caitlin squealed, stepping out of the cubbyhole. "Are you sure? Give it to me."

Lily's arm brushed against hers. "Where are you? I can't see anything!"

Caitlin waved both hands in front of her until she touched Lily's back. "Here, just reach out the flashlight in front of you." Running her fingers down Lily's arm, Caitlin stopped when she felt cold metal in her hand. She held her breath and pressed the button as hard as she could. Nothing. Just an empty *click, click, click*.

"Uh-oh," Caitlin said softly. She shook the flashlight, hard, whipping it back and forth. For an instant the light glimmered like a small birthday candle, then flickered out.

"Oh, no—I . . . I think the batteries are dead," Lily wailed. "I didn't put in new ones. What are we going to do now?"

"We're going to yell! Help!" Caitlin cried. "Mr. Mahoney! Joe Daniel! Mr. Giles! We're over *here*!"

Lily's voice rose louder than Caitlin had ever heard it. "Please help us! We can't see!"

"Keep quiet a second, Lily. Let's check if they heard us."

They stopped talking. Breathing hard, the two of them strained to listen. Caitlin heard a sound that had never before terrified her.

She heard the sound of silence.

CHAPTER 5

"**W**hat if we step into a hole?" Lily cried. "Mr. Mahoney said the mine shaft was fifteen hundred feet deep!"

"We're not anywhere near the shaft," Caitlin said, praying that she was right.

Lily's voice rose to a wail. *"But I can't see anything!"*

Caitlin forced herself to stay calm. "We'll just feel our way along. Slide your hand against the wall, and follow right behind me."

She remembered Mr. Mahoney saying that water trickled down the walls of the lower tunnels. Thank heavens they were inside a tunnel that was high and dry! It wouldn't have been much fun to feel their way along a damp, slippery cavern.

Lily kept making whimpery sounds that put a quiver in Caitlin's stomach. "Let's be quiet," Caitlin suggested, "so we can hear the other kids when we get close to them."

That worked—for a while. Lily stayed silent, except for her jagged breathing. But after a while, the little whimpers started again. Caitlin could tell that Lily was crying.

Say something—anything—Caitlin told herself. "I wonder what time it is now," she began.

"I'll look at my watch," Lily answered, her voice choked.

"How can you see your watch in the dark?"

"I push a little button and it lights up."

"Great!" Caitlin cried. "That'll be as good as a flashlight!"

But it wasn't—not at all. The tiny glow was just bright enough to show the time, six o'clock. But it couldn't even make a dent in the darkness.

"Six!" Lily wept. "That's when our parents are supposed to pick us up at the school. And we won't be there, because we're LOST!"

Caitlin swallowed hard. She'd been trying not to use the *L* word, shoving it back into a closed-off place in her mind. They'd just taken the wrong path, that's all. Soon they would find the little patch of light that showed where the mine entrance was. That is, if they found it in the next hour, before it became dark outside.

What if the Science Club had already gone? What if they had already left the mine to ride the minibus back to school and hadn't even noticed that the two of them were missing?

Caitlin's mother would notice when she came to the school to pick her up and Caitlin wasn't there. And then all the parents and Mr. Mahoney would hurry right back to the mine to find the girls, and everyone would be so happy to find them that Caitlin and Lily wouldn't even get into trouble. Well, maybe they'd get into a *little* trouble for not staying with the group. Just a little.

Her hand skimmed the rough rock walls as she tried to pick her way along the tunnel. The total inky blackness made her feel not exactly dizzy, but as if she might lose her balance.

Suddenly her hand hit something that rattled! "Ow! Ooh!" she cried. "What is this? There's a . . . a thing stuck to this wooden beam."

"Hair?" Lily asked, panic in her voice. "Human hair growing out of the wood?"

"No! It feels like metal, but kind of dusty on the outside." Groping in the dark, she said, "It's a tin can, I think. Remember when Mr. Mahoney said the miners nailed cans to the wooden posts? And inside the cans, he said, they put extra"—could she let herself hope?—"candles!" Her fingers groped over the jagged edge of the can. Feeling, feeling for . . .

"We're saved!" Caitlin shouted. "There's a candle in here!"

"Yea! Hurry up and light it," Lily yelled.

"Light it?" That presented another problem. They needed a match to light a candle. "Maybe, just maybe . . ." Caitlin felt around in the bottom of the can. "Yes!" she cried, lifting up a box of matches. "Once we light the candle, we'll be able to march right straight out of the mine."

But it was still pitch-dark as Caitlin fumbled with the matchbox, trying to pull open the part that was supposed to slide out. When she tugged at it, the dry old box fell apart, then crumbled in her fingers. She could hear the matches fall to the tunnel floor—*click, click, click, click, click.*

"Hold this candle, Lily, and be sure not to drop it!" Caitlin said. Kneeling, she carefully brushed her fingers across the gravel path. All she needed to find was a single match! With one, she could light the

28

candle, and once the candle was lit, she could find the other matches.

Still, it was creepy groping around the crushed-rock floor of the tunnel. Really creepy! What might be down there on the floor? The great-great-great-grandchildren of those mice that hid in the grain in the horse stable? Or, even worse, rats! Caitlin shuddered. Then, "Found one!" she cried in triumph.

"Where's the box?" Lily asked. "You need something to strike the match against."

"The box fell apart."

"Try a rock," Lily suggested. "When my dad goes camping, he lights matches on rocks."

"Okay." There were plenty of rocks around. In fact, they were surrounded by rocks—overhead, on all sides, and underneath them.

"But be careful," Lily warned. "Sometimes, if you strike the match too hard, the head breaks off."

Holding her breath, Caitlin slowly scraped the match against the tunnel wall. Nothing happened. She tried again, harder. A tiny orange dot of fire flickered, smoldered, and then flared into flame.

"Quick! The candle!" Caitlin yelled.

Both girls' hands shook so much that the flame wiggled around on all sides of the wick without taking hold. "Don't let the match go out!" Lily yelled. The flame had already started to burn Caitlin's fingers when, at last, the wick caught fire.

"We really are saved!" Caitlin exclaimed. "Now that we can see, we'll be out of this old mine in no time."

"Which way do we go?" Lily asked. "Straight ahead or backward?"

Caitlin looked ahead of her into blackness. She looked behind her into blackness. The one little flame in her hand burned straight up, making a small sphere of golden light in the inky center of the earth.

"I'm not sure," she whispered.

CHAPTER 6

"I have to sit down," Lily said, sounding tired and discouraged. "Do you know how long we've been in here? My watch says it's a quarter to eight now. When are they going to find us?"

Caitlin sank down beside Lily on the tunnel floor. She, too, was exhausted, even more than she would have expected, from all the wandering around in the dark.

A little earlier they'd eaten the snacks from their backpacks, dividing Caitlin's apple and Lily's package of peanut-butter crackers. Both of them had lots of water in their water bottles, so they weren't thirsty. But they felt incredibly tired!

Lily sighed. "I wish I was home in my own bed, with my canopy and my down comforter and my mother and dad coming in to say good night. My dad always comes in and kisses me good night, even when he gets home from work late."

Yawning, Caitlin asked, "Where does your dad work?"

"He's the accounts manager at Three Peaks Ski Resort," Lily answered. "My dad's really good at numbers. He always helps me with my math homework."

"That's nice." Caitlin leaned her head against the rock wall and half closed her eyes.

"Where does your father work?" Lily asked.

"I don't have a father. He left us when I was a baby." It didn't bother Caitlin too much to say that, because she couldn't remember her father at all. "My mother earns our living," she said. "She makes ski hats on her knitting machine. They're for sale in the Ski Resort gift shop. And in other places, too, not just here in Three Peaks."

"My mom stays home," Lily said. "Tonight she was going to make shrimp teriyaki for dinner." She sighed.

Caitlin and her mother just barely managed on what her mother earned. That's why they lived in a trailer home and drove an old beat-up car. Caitlin didn't mind wearing thrift-shop jeans and eating macaroni and cheese instead of shrimp teriyaki, whatever that was. She had a hundred acres of the Giles' ranch land to roam over, and a barn full of animals that Mr. Giles let her visit and pet. Plus, she had Joe Daniel Giles for her nearest neighbor and friend. That is, whenever she could get him to pay attention to her.

"I'm so tired! Maybe we should take a little nap," Lily suggested. "If we start walking again, we'll only get more lost. That'll just make it harder for my dad to find us."

"And my mom," Caitlin agreed. "But if we sleep, we better blow out the candle to save it for later." The candle had already burned down pretty far. Caitlin stared at the flame, rubbed her eyes, and stared at it again. "Am I dreaming, or is that flame getting smaller?" she asked.

Suddenly the candle sputtered out.

"You didn't have to blow it out right away," Lily said. "I hate being in the dark again."

"I didn't blow it out."

In the darkness, Caitlin could hear Lily gasp. "Maybe a ghost blew it out!"

Caitlin was just too tired right then to worry about ghosts, but Lily grabbed her arm. "Listen!" Lily whispered. "Do you hear it? What's that noise?"

Maybe Caitlin did hear something kind of faint and far away, but she couldn't be positively absolutely sure. But if she *had* heard anything, it sounded sort of like . . . crying.

"Just before the candle went out, I thought I s-s-saw something white moving around way over there," Lily stammered in Caitlin's ear.

"Just your imagination," Caitlin told her, yawning so widely that it felt as if her jaws would crack. "Oh, I'm so sleepy."

"Or else, it might have been the lady on the white horse." Lily clutched Caitlin. "I hear the sound again!"

This time, Caitlin heard it, too. Crying! Definitely crying. Caitlin stopped in mid-yawn. She clamped her mouth shut and opened her eyes wide. But there was nothing to see in the total darkness.

"It's that ghost woman! She's . . . she's weeping for her d-d-dead husband," Lily said, her voice shaking. "And she's coming closer to us. Do you hear her?"

Gripping each other tightly, the girls stayed totally silent for what seemed like dozens of minutes but was probably much less. Suddenly, Caitlin felt something brush against her face. She screamed.

"Caitlin! What is it?"

"It's hair! I felt it! The hair of the dead miners that

33

grows out of the wood!" At that same instant, Caitlin heard the cry again. This time it was right next to her. She froze in terror until she realized that the sound wasn't as much a cry as a . . . *meow*!

"*Meow, meow!*" Once again the hairy thing brushed up against her. Caitlin grabbed it. "A tail!" she exclaimed. "It's a cat's tail!"

"*Me-ow!*" the cat complained, nipping Caitlin's fingers just a little bit to make her let go of its tail.

"You mean the ghost of a cat," Lily said through chattering teeth. "One of the ones that caught the mice in the horse stable."

Caitlin said, "This cat is no ghost. Feel it, Lily! It's a real live animal. How did it get in here?" Since the candle had gone out, she couldn't see the cat at all, but still, it felt good to have something warm and alive purring around her feet.

"It wants to be petted," Caitlin said. "Look! When I rub its fur, I see sparks in the dark."

"Then it really is a ghost cat!" Lily cried. "Don't touch it!"

"The sparks are just static electricity," Caitlin said, running the palm of her hand up and down the cat's side. "It's like when you slide your feet across a carpet and then touch metal."

"Oh." Lily took a deep breath. Then, "Hey! The cat's pulling the scarf from my hair! Make it stop!"

But the cat, which seemed able to see in the dark much better than the girls could, had grabbed the silk scarf with its paws. It began to play with it.

"Wow! Look at that! More sparks," Caitlin said. She rubbed the scarf across the cat's back, causing tiny flashes of static electricity.

"It must be someone's pet, because it feels like it gets plenty to eat. But what's it doing here?" Caitlin yawned again.

"Light the candle, Caitlin," Lily told her, "so I can see it."

Caitlin had managed to pick up five matches from the tunnel floor after she'd found the candle. She'd used one for the candle. That left four in the pocket of her denim jacket. "Okay," she said now. But when she struck the first match on the rock wall, it sputtered and went out.

"Try again," Lily said.

The next match flared, burned for a few seconds, and went out, too, as if invisible fingers had snuffed it out.

"The matches won't light." Suddenly, the cat turned and scampered away. Caitlin got an idea.

"Lily, that cat must know how to get in and out of the mine. We could follow it."

"Light the candle then, Caitlin, so we can see where it's going."

Once more Caitlin tried to strike a match. Once more the match fizzled out. "They just won't light anymore!" she wailed. "But I know what we can do— maybe. We'll tie your scarf around the cat. Then, when it runs to the cave entrance, we can follow the sparks."

"It'll never work," Lily cried. "Let's just stay here and take a nap until we're rescued." She leaned her head on Caitlin's shoulder. Just then the cat came back to wrap itself around Caitlin's feet.

"I'm going to try it anyway," Caitlin said. "Here, kitty," she called, "how would you like a nice silk bow around your neck? You'll look so pretty!"

The cat meowed and didn't seem to mind being

decorated. This *has* to be someone's pet, Caitlin thought. It's so tame and friendly! Mr. Giles's barn cats would never let Caitlin handle them this way.

Lily murmured, "I want my scarf back. I bet we won't see any sparks at all. Maybe the cat doesn't even know the way out."

Caitlin tried to sound patient, but she was getting weary. "If it doesn't work, we'll sit down and wait. Look, Lily, I already see some sparks. It's so dark here that even if there aren't many, we can see them enough to follow the cat. Let's at least try!"

"Please, I just want to stay here and sleep."

"Well, I want to follow him. Go, kitty," Caitlin said. "Go home." She clambered up and pulled Lily to her feet. "Hurry up! You're right, I can hardly see the sparks, but I hear the meows, and they're moving away fast!"

Each time Caitlin and Lily thought they'd lost the cat for good, it came back again to be petted. Lily was right—the sparks were almost impossible to follow. But luckily, the cat was a great meower. "That is one chatty cat," Caitlin said.

The cat didn't seem to be taking them in any particular direction. As they twisted and turned from one passageway to the other, Lily complained, "This was a crazy idea. That cat's as lost as we are."

"At least I'm a lot wider awake now that we're moving around," Caitlin answered. Just then she tripped and landed facedown.

"What did I fall on?" she cried. She groped at the thing she'd tripped over. It felt like . . . a body!

CHAPTER 7

"Lily!" Caitlin screamed.

"Caitlin! Where are you?"

"On the floor. Something's got me!"

Arms flailing, Caitlin pushed against the heavy material. Could it be the body of a miner long dead? This thought made her try to get away all the harder. But whatever it was seemed to roll on top of her. She felt caught, like a bug in a black web. With all her strength, she cried, *Help!*

"I'm trying! I can't find you!"

Caitlin rolled to the wall. She then pulled the very last match out of her pocket and swiped it hard against the rock. The match flared. This time it stayed lit, and burned just long enough for Caitlin to see what it was on the floor.

A sleeping bag! It wasn't trying to grab her; its pull-tie had gotten caught on a button on her jacket. Every time she moved, it moved with her.

But the flare of the match showed something more, something Caitlin was so happy to see, she yelled with relief. Next to the sleeping bag lay a flashlight. She had just enough time to reach for it before the match went out.

Taking a deep breath, she lifted the flashlight and

pushed the button. A click and then . . . *light*!

It seemed as if a tiny sun had decided to rise in the mine and make it morning. She could see Lily clearly for the first time since they had gotten lost. Caitlin was surprised at how dirty and rumpled she'd become. Lily's hair, always so neatly combed, now hung in dark clumps. Her pink denim jeans were streaked with dirt; a black smudge made a stripe across her cheek.

"Where did you find the light?"

"Down there," Caitlin replied, pointing the beam of light onto a crumpled sleeping bag with a plaid flannel liner. "*That's* what I tripped over. A dumb sleeping bag." Caitlin swallowed, trying to get her voice calm again. "I . . . I thought it was a body."

"I was sure it was the ghost lady. I was scared she was grabbing you 'cause she thought you were her dead husband."

From the shadows, the cat padded to where Caitlin stood and wrapped itself between her legs. Its purrs rumbled loudly in the small, cavelike room.

"Look at the cat!" Lily exclaimed. "He's big and furry and almost *all white*. Maybe he's what I saw back there before the candle burned out. I thought it was the lady on the white horse."

With a final *meow*, the cat leaped onto the sleeping bag and curled into a fuzzy ball.

"We've got to quit getting so spooked," Caitlin announced. "You thought the cat was a ghost. I thought the sleeping bag was a dead body. Everything is the same in the dark as it is in the light. We've got to remember that."

Holding the flashlight high over her head, Caitlin peered into the makeshift room. A table hammered together from old boards stood against a jagged wall. Soda pop cans had been stacked on top of the rough boards in a brightly colored pyramid, and beneath that was a brown paper bag filled with crumpled wrappers. A plastic bucket held at least a dozen bottles of water; there was a book, a Styrofoam cooler, a tablet of paper, and a bar of soap with a tattered washcloth. A worn duffel bag had been propped up against a wall nearby.

Lily tilted back her head and looked around her. Leaning forward onto the balls of her feet, she squinted at a faraway spot. "Caitlin," she breathed. "I see a . . . deer. Underneath a tree."

"A *deer*? Are you feeling okay?"

Pointing, Lily said, "Just look."

At first Caitlin could see only dark rock and splintered beams as her flashlight danced across the wall. But then she saw it—a chalk drawing of a buckskin-colored doe, which stared at her with large eyes. Bright leaves from an aspen tree peeked out from behind the doe's back, and at her feet were two raccoons, their tails ringed in black and gray bands. Puffy white clouds drifted across a sky as blue as a robin's egg. What looked to be a hawk had been drawn in mid-flight, ready to snatch a squirrel. Where the wall met the floor lay at least fifty brightly colored pieces of chalk, all neatly lined up.

"What *is* this place?" Lily breathed. "What kind of person would draw on the walls like that?"

"I wonder what else is around here." As Caitlin turned in a small circle, the light skipped across a pile of rocks that must have caved in from the ceiling. And then, beyond the farthest shadows of the farthest wall,

40

she saw what looked like a squarish opening in the rock, like a closet with no door.

"What's that?" Lily asked.

"Maybe," Caitlin said, barely letting herself hope, "it's our way out."

Cautiously, the two girls walked to the opening. They looked down, down, down, into blackness. When Caitlin pointed the beam of light down the hole, it disappeared like a watery moonbeam.

Lily picked up a fist-sized stone and tossed it into the shaft. Five seconds went by before they heard the faraway *plink* of stone hitting metal.

"Wow," Caitlin murmured. "This must be the old hoist Mr. Giles talked about. The one the white horse disappeared from. He said the miners used it to lower hay and grain to the stable. We could ride it out of here."

"We don't know how to work it. We could end up all the way at the bottom. Mr. Mahoney said the mine's fifteen hundred feet deep."

On tiptoe, Caitlin strained to look up into the dark shaft. Old chains hung there like metal braids. Cool air blew into her face, but the smell was dank and musty.

Suddenly, Lily sucked in a breath. "Did you see that?"

"What?"

"The chain. It shook the tiniest bit."

"Are you sure?"

"Yes!" Lily said, nodding. "Just watch."

Caitlin saw it. The chains began to tremble, then move downward an inch at a time. A terrible screech echoed in the shaft, like a shrieking demon.

"Ohmigosh!" Lily cried. "Someone's coming."

Caitlin trembled, then took a step back. "That's good," she told Lily, trying to convince herself as much as her friend. "Now we'll be found, and we can go home."

"Except, is it someone good, or someone . . . bad?" Biting the side of her thumb, Lily whispered, "I'm scared."

Caitlin's heart thumped against her ribs as she took another small step back. As the seconds ticked by, she became less and less sure of being rescued. What kind of person would live in an abandoned silver mine? Why would anyone draw pictures like that? Maybe it was a robber who stored his treasure down here, just like Ali Baba and the forty thieves. Or maybe it was a murderer who dug his way out of prison and was now hiding from the police. The more Caitlin thought about it, the more her heart jumped like a jackrabbit in a cage. Her mouth grew as dry as mine dust.

"Let's leave," Lily whimpered. "We've got a flashlight now. Maybe we can find our way out all by ourselves."

Caitlin swallowed hard. Then, standing as tall as her four-foot-seven-inch frame would let her, she looked Lily squarely in the eye. "Lily, we're in trouble. There are too many tunnels down here, and we don't know which way to go. We could stay lost in this mine forever. We need to get help."

"I hope you're right," Lily said softly. "There might be worse things than being lost."

CHAPTER
8

Never before had Caitlin wanted to run as much as she did right then. The screeching of the old chains sounded like long fingernails scraping across a gigantic chalkboard. She would have put her hands over her ears if she hadn't felt so frozen with fear.

The chains shuddered, shrieking louder and louder as a four-foot-square wooden floor slowly descended in the shaft. The person who lived in this strange place was coming back, and he was about to find two strangers in his home. Was it a real human being or a ghost? Caitlin shook her head and tried to get her thinking straight. The sound was so loud that it had to be real. In moments they would know what kind of person it was.

Screech . . . screech . . . screech.

The platform lowered; two human feet in heavy black work boots appeared. The legs were planted apart like two long sticks. A little farther, and they could see a pair of jeans with the knees worn out.

Screech . . . screech . . . screech.

Now Caitlin could see the bottom hem of a denim shirt. The flashlight began to tremble in her hand; she tried to swallow, but her throat was too tight. Then Lily grabbed Caitlin in fright. The flashlight went tumbling to the ground, making wild light patterns as it fell.

Caitlin wanted to find the flashlight, but she couldn't tear her eyes away from whomever or whatever was being lowered on the platform. A torso, then thin shoulders—suddenly, a blinding light hit her right in her face. Her eyes squeezed shut against the glare.

"Oh!" Lily squealed. "It's too bright. I can't see!"

"Who are you?" a voice bellowed.

"I . . . we're sorry," Caitlin stammered.

"Who ARE you?"

"We're from the Three Peaks Science Club, and we were trying to get some rocks from the mine and—"

"What are you doing in my place?"

"I forgot my flashlight and Lily's batteries died," Caitlin chattered. She always talked extra-fast when she was scared, and this strange voice scared her a lot. "See, Pablo, he's in our Science Club, and he's always playing jokes, so we tried to get him back and we hid and—"

The words spit from the shaft like thunder. *"Get out!"*

"But—"

"Now!"

Thoughts spun through Caitlin's head like leaves in a whirlwind. They'd have to go back into the mine, but where would they end up? They would never find their way out of that endless black maze. And now the voice behind the light wouldn't help them at all, which meant she and Lily could be lost forever. They might never see their parents again. For the first time since she'd been lost, Caitlin felt tears well up in her

eyes. She missed her mom so much. Her mother must be so worried by now. All because Caitlin wanted to get back at Pablo for his joking.

"Excuse me, sir?"

The voice belonged to Lily—shy Lily, who hardly ever raised her hand at school. Lily took two steps forward. With one arm shielding her eyes from the bright light, she told him, "If we knew how to get back to our friends, we would go and leave you alone. But we're lost."

"No one can know that I'm here!"

With another step, Lily said, "If you take us back to where we started, we'll walk right out and never, ever tell anyone about you. We promise. Right, Caitlin?"

"Right!" Caitlin added quickly.

The light seemed to drop down, just a little, so that it was no longer hitting Caitlin and Lily in their faces. Caitlin could make out the outline of a head; whoever was talking to them had blond hair. He was tall, almost six feet, and as thin as a crane.

"Please—you've got to help us," Lily urged.

"Why should I? It's not that hard. You can find your own way out."

Slowly, Lily took another step. Now she was only three feet away from the man who seemed to hate having them there. "What would have happened to you if you were little like us, and you got lost?" Lily asked gently. "Wouldn't your mom have been worried about you? Wouldn't she want someone to help you go home?"

That seemed to make the difference. The blond head began to gently move up and down in a nod. "Okay," he said. "I'll take you. But it's on one condition."

"Anything! Whatever you say!" Caitlin and Lily chimed together.

"You've got to promise you'll never, ever tell who I am, or where I'm staying, or how I get in and out of this place. Do you swear?"

"We swear," Caitlin declared, raising her right hand.

"Okay. As long as you've promised, I'll let you see me."

The person walked past them and put the light on the small wooden table. Caitlin blinked once, then again. When her eyes finally adjusted, she gasped! She couldn't believe what she saw!

CHAPTER 9

"**Y**ou're not a grown-up!" Caitlin cried. Now that the light was no longer in her eyes, she could see that the person who had scared her so much was a boy barely older than Joe Daniel. He was tall and as thin as a broomstick. His clothes hung on him in loose, empty folds. It seemed to Caitlin that his hands and feet were too big for the rest of his body.

"I'm old enough. Fifteen next month. Who are you?"

"I'm Caitlin Marsh and she"—Caitlin pointed—"is Lily Kato. We got lost, and we're in lots of trouble because we were supposed to stay with the rest of our Science Club. Mr. Mahoney—that's our teacher—he's probably even called our parents by now. What's your name?"

"Tyler."

"Tyler what?" Lily asked.

"None of your business," he snapped. "My cat's name is Hairy Snowball, and that's about all you need to know." An olive-green backpack had been slung over his shoulder. Hunching, he dropped it with a thud next to the Styrofoam cooler.

"Look, I've got to unpack my stuff. It'll go bad if I don't put it on ice. Then I'll take you out. Deal?"

Tyler produced a small container of milk and a

block of orange cheese. "Breakfast and dinner for tomorrow," he said. "Plus a piece of leftover burger for Hairy. He loves this stuff." At the sound of the wrapper unfolding, Hairy slithered through Tyler's legs, forming a number eight.

"Who put that dumb bow around your neck, Hairy?" Tyler asked. "You're a *guy* cat."

Watching him pull the bow from Hairy's neck, Caitlin couldn't help but wonder about this mysterious boy. What was he doing here? Why did his last name have to be a secret? What kind of kid would choose such a dark place for a home? A thought suddenly hit Caitlin like a splash of cold water: Maybe Tyler didn't have a place to live.

Sometimes on the news she would see stories about men, women, and children who slept out on the street, without even a blanket to keep away the bitter cold. Then Caitlin's mom would say, "See, Caitlin, some people really have things tough. You and I are lucky, sweetie." And Caitlin would look around her trailer home—at her snug bed and her cheery kitchen—and wish that no one ever had to live without a home.

What if Tyler were one of those people she saw on television? What if he were really and truly alone? The next words came out of Caitlin's mouth before she could think them all the way through. "Tyler, are you an orphan? Is that why you have to stay in the mine?"

Tyler handed the silk scarf to Lily and frowned at Caitlin. His eyes, which were the same color as his blue jeans, widened.

"What? An orphan?"

"'Cause if you are, you could come home with

me." As soon as she closed her mouth, Caitlin wished she could take the words back. Her mother wouldn't even let her keep a stray cat, let alone a stray boy.

"Me, too. You could stay in our house—it's big," Lily offered. "You shouldn't live in a place where it's night all the time."

A smile tugged at the corner of Tyler's lips. "Don't worry about me—I got parents." He stared at the wall behind Caitlin's head, deep in thought. "I've been gone three weeks today. Bet they don't even miss me."

"Did you run away 'cause they were mean to you?" Caitlin asked.

Shrugging, Tyler said, "Sort of. My dad made me do all kinds of chores on our ranch. He hated it when I took time out to draw, which is what I love to do most. We fought all the time, especially this past year. Then, a couple weeks ago, most of our sheep got out of their pen. One of them got killed."

"Oh, no," Caitlin whispered. She knew how important sheep were to the ranchers who raised them. Losing sheep was serious business. "How did they get out?"

Tyler pinched his lips together. "I . . . I guess it was my fault. I was supposed to fix the fence. But the light was perfect, and I wanted to get my drawing just right. So I didn't work on the fence and the sheep . . . Well, anyway, when my dad found out, he was yellin' so loud that I just lost it and told him off. Then I packed my bags and blew out. Found a job sweepin' floors at Burger Blaster." Tyler pulled a coil of hair from his face and tucked it behind one ear. "I'm never goin' back home."

Softly, Lily asked, "Do you like it in here?"

It took a minute for Tyler to answer. "Being on my

own is harder than I thought. Most of the time I'm slingin' burgers, and then when I get back I'm too tired to draw much. Got to live here 'cause I can't afford anywhere else. So now it's just me and Hairy. We like it that way, don't we, Hairy?"

The cat purred.

"Aren't you scared of spirits of the dead miners and the lady on the white horse?" Caitlin asked. She'd hate to sleep in such a dark place.

"I'm a lot more scared of runnin' out of money."

Caitlin thought about the rocky walls and the endless maze of tunnels. She couldn't imagine being here, all alone, forever. What a sad life. There's more than one way, Caitlin decided, for a person to become a ghost.

"Can't you go home?" Lily asked.

"Nah, it's too late. Besides, I doubt they'd want me back, and I'm not goin' to ask. You guys are too little to understand."

"But—"

"Forget it!" Tyler's sharp reply cut off Lily's protest like a knife. "Now get on the platform, and I'll pull you up. It's time for you to go home."

CHAPTER
10

Riding up on the wooden platform was almost fun. The screeching wasn't scary at all, now that Lily and Caitlin knew what caused it. Best of all, though, was reaching the top, when Tyler pushed open a creaky gate and they stepped out onto dirt and grass under the night sky. Caitlin gulped deep breaths of delicious fresh air. Then she turned toward the valley beneath them.

"Wow! Look down there," she exclaimed. "Something's happening."

Far down the hill, red and blue lights flashed on half a dozen police cars. The Three Peaks Volunteer Fire Brigade truck was parked close to the mine entrance, where firemen in yellow coats waited, holding stretchers. On another large truck, a tall pole held four bright spotlights that illuminated the area like a football field, making it almost as bright as day. Dozens of ordinary people clustered in groups of two and three or more. Behind a barricade, more people waited. All of them were looking toward the opening of the mine.

"There must be an emergency," Lily said. "I wonder what happened? Look, there's a TV truck, and people pointing cameras, and—"

"Don't you get it?" Tyler asked them. "All that is about you!"

"Huh?" Caitlin's mouth dropped open in astonishment. "About us?"

"Sure!" Tyler swept his arm to indicate the crowds of people, the uniformed officers, and all the emergency vehicles. "You kids got lost in the mine. They're all trying to find you. See the ambulances? They think you might be hurt."

"Ohmigosh! Ohmigosh!" Caitlin said it over and over. "Lily, we are in *huge* trouble!"

Lily began to cry. "I don't care—I want my mom and dad. Do you think they're down there?" She took a few steps downhill in the dark.

"Wait, Lily," Caitlin cried, throwing out her arm to stop her friend. "It's not safe. You might fall. Tyler needs to take us down to show us the path." Of course, that wasn't true. Caitlin could climb up and down trails like a mountain goat, in the daylight or the dark. But she worried that if they left without Tyler, he might just run away again. He might go somewhere else where no one would ever find him. His next words proved her right.

"I'm not going down there," he announced. "Too many people."

Caitlin had to think fast to find a way to convince him. "Tyler, please don't make us go alone! It's too dark, and the mountain's so steep that we could fall and get *killed*!"

Tyler hesitated.

"Just take us partway down the mountain," Caitlin pleaded, "and then you can turn around and go back, and we'll never tell anyone who you are or where you are, like we promised." And that, at least, was true. She would keep her word to Tyler not to tell anyone, but she hadn't promised not to trick him into being found.

55

"Okay. Just partway," he agreed, reluctantly.

Lily really did need Tyler's help descending the mountain path. She wasn't nearly as sure-footed as Caitlin. She held tightly to his arm and took small, uncertain steps.

Halfway down, Tyler said, "This is far enough. You can make it the rest of the way on your own."

This time it was Lily who begged him, "Don't leave us yet, Tyler. My shoes are slippery. Just a little farther. Please!"

"Oh, all right." They'd almost reached the bottom when Tyler announced, "Okay, I quit. See you later—in some other life!"

"Grab his arm, Lily!" Caitlin cried as she held fast to Tyler's other hand. Then, "Hey! Over here!" she yelled.

One of the big spotlights turned right on them, illuminating the three of them and nearly blinding their eyes.

"There they are! They're safe!" Cheers and shouts went up from the crowds of people, who started running toward them. Tyler tried to get away. But by then the first wave of people had reached them and was shouting things like "Are you okay?" and "Are you hurt?" and "Get the medics up here!" Tyler became lost in the crowd.

"We're okay, we're really okay," Caitlin tried to tell them. The next thing she knew she was in her mother's arms, being squeezed so tightly she could hardly catch her breath. Her mother was crying in great big sobs that made Caitlin cry, too.

"Am I in big trouble?" Caitlin whispered in her mother's ear, as flashes from reporters' cameras popped all around them. A TV person shoved a microphone toward their faces. When Caitlin lifted her

head from her mother's shoulder, she saw that Lily and her parents were being mobbed the same way.

"I'm just so happy to see you!" her mother answered, her voice all choked with tears. "Oh, sweetheart, I was so scared! Are you all right?"

"I'm just . . . tired."

Now that Caitlin was safe, she couldn't believe how much she wanted to snuggle into her own warm bed and go to sleep.

Pulling Caitlin into another giant hug, her mother said, "Let's get you home now. We'll put you into a nice, hot bath and I'll make you—"

"Wait, Mom." Caitlin pulled away for a moment, because she wanted to find Tyler and make sure he was all right. Standing on tiptoe, she strained to see, but so many people and the glare of the lights made it hard to find anyone. She saw Lily, wedged between her parents, getting into their shiny white car. Mr. Mahoney, wearing a grin as big as Christmas day, was talking to a group of reporters. It took Caitlin a moment before she realized that Tyler was gone. Sighing, she took her mother's hand.

"Ready now, honey?" her mother asked.

"I'm ready," Caitlin said, winding her arms around her mother's neck. "I want to go home."

CHAPTER
11

"I think you girls were punished enough," Mr. Mahoney said at the next Science Club meeting. It didn't take place the day after they'd been found but on the next day after that. Both Lily and Caitlin had missed school following their rescue, just to catch up on sleep and to let their folks hug them a lot.

"What do you think, kids?" Mr. Mahoney asked the Science Club members. "Shall we let them off without any further reprimand?"

"Yeah, sure, you bet," everyone agreed. Caitlin stayed silent because she wasn't sure what "reprimand" was, the thing that Mr. Mahoney was going to let them off without any further—whatever!

"Thank you," Lily said meekly.

Sun streamed through the windows of the school library, where the Science Club held its meetings. From now on, and as long as she lived, Caitlin knew she would be grateful for sky and sunlight and bright colors.

"So how many ghosts did you see in the mine?" Pablo asked, jumping around in his seat.

"None," Caitlin answered. "Lily thought the white cat was the ghost woman on the white horse. But it wasn't. I thought the cat's tail was the hair growing

59

out of the wooden beams. But it wasn't. And then I thought the sleeping bag was a dead body, and that wasn't true, either."

"You see, boys and girls," Mr. Mahoney said, "spooky things can always be explained."

Pablo looked disappointed, until Lily said, "Except . . ."

"What? What?" Pablo and Reese both cried. "Except what, Lily?"

"We were there in the dark," Lily said softly, "sitting down because we were both soooo tired. Suddenly, the candle just . . . went out."

"You mean a ghost blew it out?" Reese asked, leaning forward eagerly.

"What else could it be?" Lily answered. "And you want to know what else? Caitlin couldn't get the matches to light, either. Not while we were sitting there."

"How come?" Pablo asked.

"I don't know. Every time she tried to strike a match, it went out, like somebody, or some*thing*, blew it out. And there wasn't a breeze or anything."

"And then," Caitlin broke in, "after we left that spot and followed the cat out a ways, the very last match burned just fine. Maybe a spirit didn't want us there. Maybe that was the spot where he . . . died."

"Oh, no! Oh, no!" Everyone grew silent as Mr. Mahoney gripped the desk with his hands. He turned as pale as the sheets of paper stacked in front of him. "You say you both felt sleepy, back where the candle wouldn't light?"

"Awfully sleepy. I couldn't stop yawning," Caitlin agreed. Just remembering it made her yawn again. "Like that," she said.

Mr. Mahoney whipped off his wire-framed glasses and took some deep breaths.

"What's wrong, Mr. Mahoney?" Caitlin asked. "Do you think it really was a ghost that blew out the candle and the matches?"

"No." Mr. Mahoney opened his mouth and moved his lips, but the words seemed stuck inside. After a moment, he said, "You were in a pocket of dead air."

"How can air be dead?" Kevin Running Fox asked.

His voice shaky, Mr. Mahoney answered, "When all or most of the oxygen is gone from air, it's called 'dead.' That's the reason you felt so tired, Lily and Caitlin. Because everyone needs oxygen to breathe. And a flame needs oxygen to burn—that's why the matches wouldn't light. If you girls hadn't moved from that place, you might not have survived!"

Caitlin shivered. "So Hairy Snowball saved our lives."

"Who's Hairy Snowball?" they all wanted to know.

"That's what Tyler called his cat. He's all white, and he's got just about the thickest fur I ever saw on a cat." Suddenly, Caitlin clapped her hand over her mouth. Until now, she'd been careful not to mention Tyler. Not to anyone. And she'd just broken her promise!

"Is Tyler the name of the kid who led you out of the mine?" Chantelle Landers asked.

Caitlin's eyes widened. She looked at Lily, who shook her head softly. She seemed as puzzled as Caitlin.

"How did you know about Tyler?" Caitlin asked.

61

"Oh, he was on the news last night. Didn't you watch?"

"No. I was way too tired."

"Girl, it was something," Chantelle said, her face brightening. "Tyler's mom and dad were in the crowd the night you got lost. When they saw Tyler, they grabbed him and hugged him and cried and everything. The cameras caught it all. He's back home now."

Reese nodded. "Channel Six even showed some stuff he drew on the walls inside the mine. They're saying he's a really good artist. Maybe they'll make a TV movie out of his story, and I"—he jerked his thumb to his chest—"can play the lead."

"So the cat saved you and you saved Tyler," Chantelle added.

"Yeah. We followed Hairy Snowball away from that—that place where we were so sleepy." Suddenly, Caitlin's eyes widened and she slumped hard into a chair. The meaning of Mr. Mahoney's words hit her. She and Lily had come close to falling asleep . . . forever!

"Mr. Mahoney," Caitlin said fervently, reaching for his hand, "I promise I will *never, never, never* break a rule again."

"And I don't think I'll ever take you kids anywhere again without a whole *busload* of chaperons," Mr. Mahoney said, still shaky.

"And on the next field trip," Joe Daniel added, "I'll be your partner, Caitlin, so I can watch over you and keep you out of trouble."

When Caitlin heard that, she had to smile. All the awful stuff—being lost, scared out of her wits, and worried over what was going to happen to her because she'd broken the rules—well, it might have been worth it, at least just the tiniest little bit. Because Joe Daniel cared about her.

And *that* was worth a lot!

VISIT PLANET TROLL

A super-sensational spot on the Internet
at http://www.troll.com

Check out Kids' T-Zone, a really cool place where you can...

- Play games!
- Win prizes!
- Speak your mind in the Voting Voice Box!
- Find out about the latest and greatest books and authors!
- Shop at BookWorld!
- Order books on-line!

And a UNIVERSE more of GREAT BIG FUN!

To order a free Internet trial with CompuServe's Internet access service, Sprynet,
adults may call 1-888-947-2669. (For a limited time only.)